To Sandra and Tim
—*M. D.*

For Olivia.
Thanks to Kimberly Berry, Deen City Farm,
and Deanhills Stud for all their help.
—*A. R.*

Margaret K. McElderry Books
An imprint of Simon & Schuster Children's Publishing Division
1230 Avenue of the Americas, New York, New York, 10020
Text copyright © 2008 by Malachy Doyle
Illustrations copyright © 2008 by Angelo Rinaldi
First published in Great Britain in 2008 by Simon & Schuster UK Ltd.
First U.S. edition, 2008
All rights reserved, including the right of reproduction in whole or in part in any form.
The text for this book is set in Minister.
The illustrations are rendered in oil paint on canvas.
Book design by Genevieve Webster
Manufactured in China
2 4 6 8 10 9 7 5 3 1
CIP data for this book is available from the Library of Congress.
ISBN-13: 978-1-4169-2467-8
ISBN-10: 1-4169-2467-1

By winter, his coat is thick and sleek.
The colt grows bigger and stronger every day,
kicking up the snow with his hooves
as he charges around the paddock.

Then, one fine spring morning,
the girl offers him a carrot.
As the yearling leans forward,
she slips a rope around his neck
and puts a head collar over his warm,
silken nose.

Stroking his head, talking softly,
the girl leads him quietly around the field.
"You're such a beautiful horse," she tells him.

"One day we're going to ride, you and I,
over the hill and all the way to the sea. . . ."